# THE PEACEABLE KINGDOM

STORY BY EWA ZADRZYNSKA   ILLUSTRATIONS BY TOMEK OLBINSKI
PAINTING FROM THE BROOKLYN MUSEUM

M.M. ART BOOKS, INC., NEW YORK

M.M. Art Books, Inc.

510 East 80th Street

New York, New York 10021


Text copyright © 1993 by Ewa Zadrzynska

Illustrations copyright © 1993 by Tomek Olbinski

Compilation copyright © M.M. Art Books, Inc.

Library of Congress Cataloging-in-Publication Data 93-086631

Ewa Zadrzynska: The Peaceable Kingdom


Designed by Michael M. Glowacki

Edited by Frances Foster

Distributed by Publishers Group West

4065 Hollis Street, Emeryville, CA 94608

Tel. 1 800 788-3123

Printed in Hong Kong


ISBN # 0-9638904-0-9

FOR ZUZA AND DANIELA

–E. Z.

One moonlit Saturday night, while the whole city slept, the door of the big gray building at the corner of Washington Avenue and Eastern Parkway in Brooklyn, New York, opened, and something with huge yellow eyes stepped outside.

A moment later the door opened again and another pair of big yellow eyes emerged from the building. Then a pair of medium-sized yellow eyes slipped out and joined the strange yellow-eyed couple.

They, whoever they were, looked around cautiously. All was quiet. Slowly they started walking down Eastern Parkway. They had gone only a short distance when a single car drove by. The car's lights shone on them, and the driver honked his horn in panic. The yellow-eyed trio, surprised by the bright headlights and the honking sound, jumped over a high iron fence, not far from the big gray building.

On Sunday morning when the first visitors came to the Brooklyn Botanic Garden they saw a very strange sight. There, in the middle of a meadow, surrounded by pink and white azalea bushes, stood a huge lion, a spotted leopard, and a gray wolf. The lion was shaking with fear as an angry pigeon swooped over his head; the leopard was nervously licking his paw while three mocking squirrels chattered at him, showing their sharp teeth; the wolf, surrounded by ten warrior-like frogs, closed his eyes and huddled close to the lion and the leopard.

"Mother, look, a lion!" shouted a five-year-old boy called Brian, whose big glasses had slipped down to the end of his nose.

"Mother, a leopard! Look at the leopard!" screamed Susan, Brian's seven-year-old sister, whose freckled cheeks turned red from excitement.

"Don't move, children!" said their mother and she grabbed their hands.

"They're beautiful and they're scared," said Susan. "We have to help them."

"Watch out. They'll devour you in a second," cried an elderly woman who held a pink umbrella over her head to keep the sunshine off her pale skin. "Whoever let those wild beasts in here should be arrested. This is not the zoo. This is the Botanic Garden."

"How incredible!" said a security guard, as he called the police.

The police came immediately. They circled the wild beasts and cocked their guns, ready to fire. The animals stared at the guns, at the navy-blue hats, at the big police boots, and drew closer together. A tear of sadness fell from the lion's eyes. He tried to hide it with his paw, but the leopard noticed and right away shed his own two tears of sadness. When the wolf saw the leopard's wet eyes he burst into tears himself.

"Don't shoot!" ordered the mayor, who had come with more police. "First, we must find out what's happened."

"Yes, let's investigate," said the two television crews and the four newspaper reporters who had just arrived. Then came firefighters and three famous professors. Everyone was talking at once.

"Dangerous animals in the garden!" "Who let them in?" "Who is responsible?" "Where did they come from?"

"In my city, predators are simply not allowed in botanic gardens. We must do something about it," said the mayor.

The firefighters raised their hoses. "We can frighten them away," they said.

"Wait a minute," said the mayor. "You will scare away the garden wildlife, the birds, squirrels, butterflies and bees. And don't forget the children. Let's ask the professors what should be done."

The professors were scrutinizing the yellow-eyed beasts with their scientific tools, (magnifying glasses, binoculars, and calipers) and leafing through their wildlife encyclopedias.

"This one must be a lion," said the famous New York professor. "But if he was truly a lion he would surely have eaten this pigeon."

"I've seen hundreds of leopards but never one that is afraid of squirrels," said the famous California professor, sagely.

And the third one said: "I'm a world-famous professor and I am telling you, a real wolf would have finished off these frogs, but this one is afraid of small green creatures who don't even have sharp teeth or long claws. All they can do is spit."

Everybody agreed that something strange was going on in the Brooklyn Botanic Garden.

"Maybe these animals came from Mars," offered the New York professor. The four reporters wrote that down.

"Maybe they came from the ocean," observed the professor from California. The four reporters wrote that down, too.

"I know," said the world-famous professor. "They must have come from the Prospect Park Children's Zoo."

"Impossible. I have a feeling they belong to the Bronx Zoo," the New York professor spoke up again.

"Well, let's call the zoo," the four reporters shouted at the same time, putting aside their pens.

But the Bronx Zoo staff counted all their lions, leopards, and wolves, and none was missing.

"They might have come from the circus," someone suggested. But there was no circus in the city at the moment.

"Action! We need action. In my city there is no place for a stray lion, leopard, and wolf," the mayor declared with authority. The police officers raised their guns higher and the firefighters aimed their hoses.

"Stop!" screamed Brian, whose glasses had slipped again to the end of his nose. "Let me have another look."

He took off his glasses, wiped them carefully, and put them back on. "I know these animals. They are from *The Peaceable Kingdom*."

"The Peaceable Kingdom? Where's that?" asked the four reporters.

"Right there." Brian pointed to the big gray building. The four reporters were about to write that down in their notebooks when the first professor said: "Impossible."

"Nonsense," said the second professor.

"What does a child know about such matters," said the third professor.

"My brother is right. I was there with him. I remember these animals, too," said Brian's sister, Susan, as her freckled cheeks blushed pink.

At that moment, one of the police officers noticed animal footprints on the grass.

"Let's follow these tracks. Surely they'll lead us to the animals' residence," she said.

"Let's go!" ordered the mayor.

All the firefighters and police, the four reporters and three professors, the security guard, and all the parents with their children fell in line behind the mayor.

The tracks ended by the high fence. On the other side of the fence was a sidewalk. The world-famous professor looked up at the sky, as though checking to see if the animals might have fallen from the heavens. The famous California professor looked down, as though hunting for signs that they had emerged from underground. The New York professor became thoughtful and stared at the sidewalk. On the gray concrete he spotted red prints of a lion's left forepaw.

"Look!" he cried. "Let's follow these prints!"

The prints ended by an overturned can of red paint near a freshly painted standpipe, just in front of the entrance to the big gray building.

"I can't believe it! This is the Brooklyn Museum," said the famous New York professor.

"It must be a joke. Wild animals don't live in art museums," said the famous California professor.

"Ladies and gentlemen, I think we are wasting our time," said the world-famous professor.

"It's possible, but let's waste a few minutes more," said the mayor as Brian opened the door.

"Follow me, please!" said Brian. He guided them through a big hall straight to the staircase in the back. He climbed up four floors and stopped on the fifth.

"*The Peaceable Kingdom* is here," he said.

There were many paintings and many sculptures but *The Peaceable Kingdom* was nowhere to be seen. The three professors looked at the mayor.

"The kids fooled us!" the three of them said at the same moment.

"No, we didn't!" cried Susan, pointing to the inscription above the entrance to another big room. "*The Peaceable Kingdom* is in the American Painting and Sculpture room." She entered the room so confidently that even the three professors followed her.

Susan was right. *The Peaceable Kingdom,* a painting by Edward Hicks, was there. On the right side of the picture a few cows grazed peacefully; behind them other animals rested. The animals seemed relaxed, but their eyes were sad. The eyes of the three children who stood among the animals were even sadder. In the background, on the left side of the painting, Governor William Penn was signing a peace treaty with the American Indians. The peacemakers were so occupied with making peace that they didn't notice anything else, certainly not the sadness surrounding them.

"I get the impression that something is wrong," said the mayor, looking at the painted children and animals.

"Yes," the Painted Girl spoke up.

"We used to have a lion, a leopard, and a wolf. But when we woke up this morning they were gone."

"We're afraid somebody stole them," cried the two Painted Boys.

"Nobody stole your animals," said the world-famous professor. "They are only half a block away, in the Botanic Garden."

"Really?" all the Painted Children exclaimed at the same moment.

"You should come with us and bring them back into the frame."

"That's impossible. We can't leave the painting," said the Painted Girl.

"You have my permission," said the mayor.

"And ours," said the police officers.

"Our duty is to stay here, the way Mr. Hicks painted us," answered the Painted Children.

"I'm sure Mr. Hicks would be upset to learn that some of the animals are out of his painting," said Susan, blushing.

"He would be even more upset if he knew how frightened his animals are," said Brian, whose glasses slipped to the end of his nose once more.

"Oh! Do you think so?" asked the Painted Girl. And without waiting for an answer she jumped out of the frame. The two Painted Boys followed her.

Brian and Susan led everybody back to the Botanic Garden, where the lion, the leopard, and the wolf still huddled together in the middle of the lawn.

When the lion saw the Painted Children he jumped with joy. The leopard and the wolf immediately joined him.

"What happened?" asked the Painted Girl.

"It's not my fault," said the wolf. "I always do what the leopard does."

"Don't blame me. All my life I have followed the lion," said the leopard.

"You should blame me or, rather, Mr. Hicks," said the lion. "It was Mr. Hicks who believed that one day there would be peace all over the world. I thought we had been in our frame long enough for peace to have come to earth. I wanted to see it with my own eyes. What I saw instead was a big monster that honked at us, little animals that bit the leopard, green creatures that spit on the wolf, and a pigeon that tried to peck out my eyes. Even the people threatened us.... I want to go back to our peaceable kingdom."

"So do I," said the leopard, who always copied the lion.

"And I do too," added the wolf, echoing the leopard.

"We want to go home," cried the lion, the leopard, and the wolf all at once, bursting into tears one after the other. They cried so sadly that the pigeon, the frogs, the squirrels, and even the butterflies joined in.

Soon the whole garden was crying. Even the worm, who had never shed a tear in his whole life, had brimming eyes.

He had to wipe them with his tail so he could watch the other animals weep.

Walking down the nearby lane, two field mice, longtime residents of the Brooklyn Botanic Garden, stopped to give out a thin, weak whine, although they didn't know why.

Susan's and Brian's eyes overflowed with tears. When the mayor saw the children and animals crying, he started to cry himself. When the police officers saw the mayor crying, they cried too. Then the firefighters began to cry, and then the two TV crews and the four newspaper reporters. The three professors were the last to join the weeping crowd.

The animals and the people cried until they had no more tears. When they had finished, everybody started to kiss everybody else. The frogs kissed the wolf, the squirrels kissed the leopard, and the pigeon kissed the lion.

"This feels like home," said the lion. The leopard and the wolf nodded in agreement.

The world-famous professor wiped his tears, looked in his encyclopedia, and said: "Wait a minute. Mr. Hicks painted you in 1835. I think it's still too soon to expect the peaceable kingdom to have come to earth."

The lion became thoughtful. "But why is it too soon?" he asked.

"I wish we knew the answer to that," said the mayor. "All I know is that when we are kind to each other the world seems a much nicer place."

"I will do my best," said Brian, whose glasses slipped down to the end of his nose, as usual.

"Me, too," said Susan, as her cheeks turned red.

"So will we," said the firefighters, the police officers, the professors, the parents, and the mayor. The newspaper reporters and the television crews were too busy recording this unusual talk to say anything.

"Well, I think your place is in your painting in the Brooklyn Museum," said the mayor, looking at the lion. The police officers and the firefighters nodded. The two television crews and the four reporters nodded as well. The three famous professors were the last to agree.

"You are absolutely right," said the lion.

"Let's go," said the Painted Girl.

So the Painted Children led the way. They were followed by Susan with the wolf. Then came Brian and the leopard. The lion went on his own, proudly swinging his huge head from side to side. Behind the lion came the mayor and the three professors with their tools and books. The police officers and the firefighters left, while the two TV crews filmed everything and the four reporters started to write the headlines about this strange Sunday morning in Brooklyn, New York.

Back in the museum the lion jumped into the picture frame. The leopard and then the wolf followed him. The Painted Children thanked everybody for their help, kissed Brian and Susan, and then found their places among the animals, just as Mr. Hicks had painted them.

And all was well in *The Peaceable Kingdom.*

*The Peaceable Kingdom, The Brooklyn Museum, Brooklyn, New York*

Variations of *The Peaceable Kingdom* painted by Edward Hicks can be seen in the following museums and collections:

1. *Yale University Art Gallery, New Haven, Connecticut*

2. *Abby Aldrich Rockefeller Folk Art Center, Williamsburg, Virginia*

3. *Friends Historical Library of Swarthmore College, Pennsylvania*

4. *Museum of Fine Arts, Houston, Texas*

5. *San Antonio Museum Association, San Antonio, Texas*

6. *National Gallery of Art, Washington, D.C.*

7. *Phillips Collection, Washington, D.C.*

8. *Metropolitan Museum of Art, New York, New York*

9. *Albright-Knox Gallery, Buffalo, New York*

10. *Everson Gallery of Art, Syracuse, New York*

11. *New York State Historical Association, Cooperstown, New York*

12. *Dallas Museum of Fine Arts, Dallas, Texas*

13. *Denver Museum of Art, Denver, Colorado*

14. *Cleveland Museum of Art, Cleveland, Ohio*

15. *Nelson Atkins Museum, Kansas City, Missouri*

16. *Mercer Museum, Bucks County, Pennsylvania*

17. *Philadelphia Museum of Art, Philadelphia, Pennsylvania*

18. *Carnegie Institute Museum of Art, Pittsburgh, Pennsylvania*

Edward Hicks was a Quaker preacher who lived in Pennsylvania from 1780 to 1830. During his life he preached about his dream that the world could become peaceful and happy, as promised by the prophet Isaiah in the Old Testament. Isaiah foretold that The Peaceable Kingdom, where lions would eat grass, wolves would play with sheep, and even little children would be safe among wild beasts, would come to earth one day. And then nobody would know harm and violence or know what unhappiness and trouble mean.

Later in his life Edward Hicks took brushes to canvas and started to paint his vision of this world. He painted it again and again, and today there are more than fifty versions of his *Peaceable Kingdom*, many of them hanging in museums. *The Peaceable Kingdom* shown in this book hangs in the Brooklyn Museum.

The Peaceable Kingdom as described in the eleventh chapter of the prophet Isaiah, in the Old Testament: One day the world will be so peaceful that. *"The wolf shall dwell with the lamb, and the leopard shall lie down with the kid, and the calf and the lion and the fatling together and a little child shall lead them."*